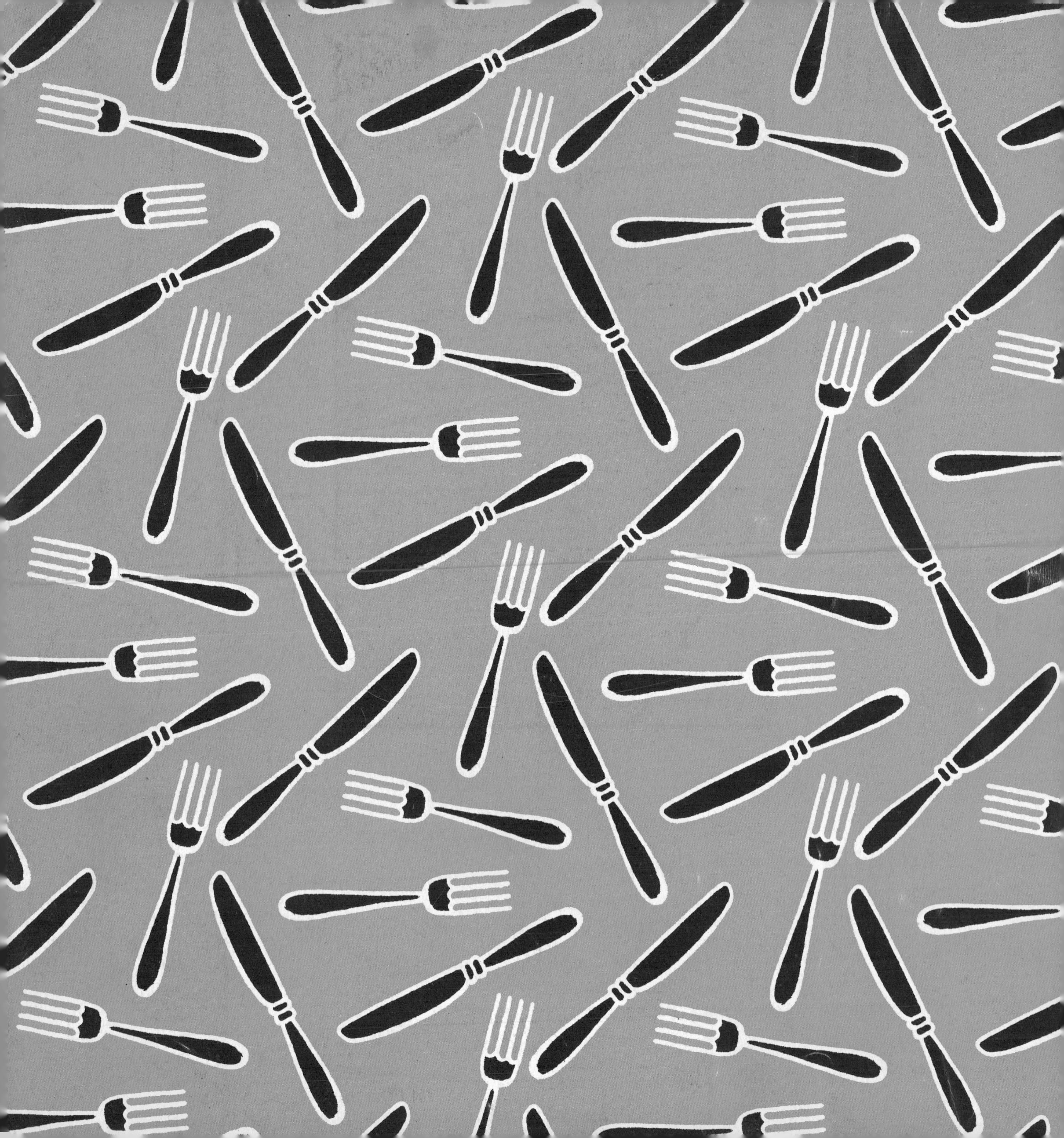

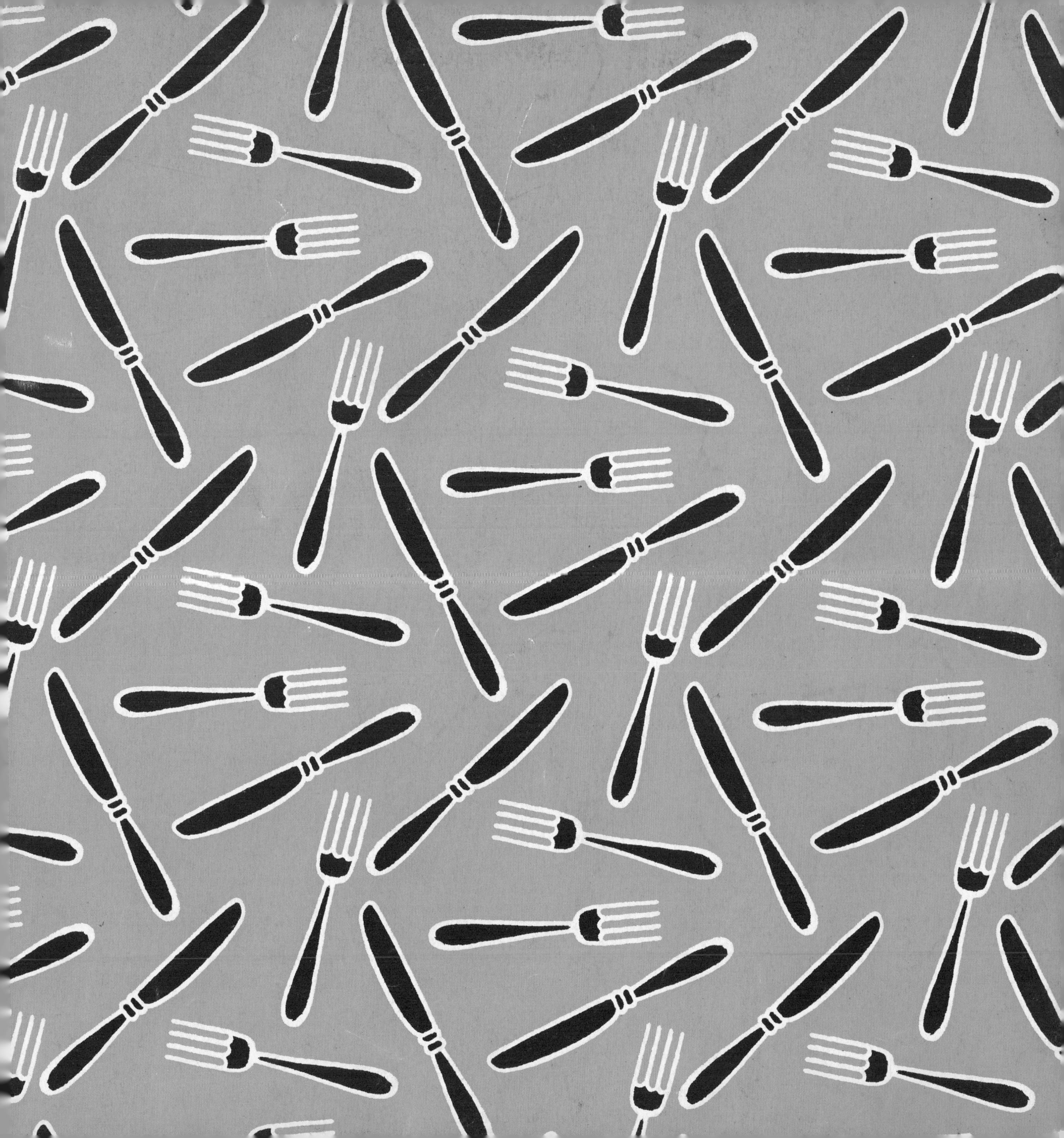

To Claire, Chloe, Kathryn and Rosie - N.G. and E.P.

For Florence - N.S.

First published 2007 by Macmillan Children's Books
This edition published 2008 by Macmillan Children's Books
a division of Macmillan Publishers Limited
20 New Wharf Road, London N1 9RR
Basingstoke and Oxford
Associated companies throughout the world
www.panmacmillan.com

ISBN: 978-0-230-01616-3

1 3 5 7 9 8 6 4 2

A CIP catalogue for this book is available from the British Library.

Printed in Belgium by Proost

NEVER use a KNIFE and FORK

Written by Neil Goddard

from an original idea by Elizabeth Perry

Illustrated by Nick Sharratt

MACMILLAN CHILDREN'S BOOKS

Never use a knife and fork.

Stuff your mouth till you can't talk!

Soak your pigtails in your soup.

Squish your
fishcake
into gloop.
Tomato
Sauce

Slosh your squash
around your cup.

Use your sleeves to mop it up.

Suck
ice-cream
from
underneath.

Scrape your

biscuit

with your teeth.

Squirt your
yoghurt
from the pot.

Tie your Sausage in a knot.

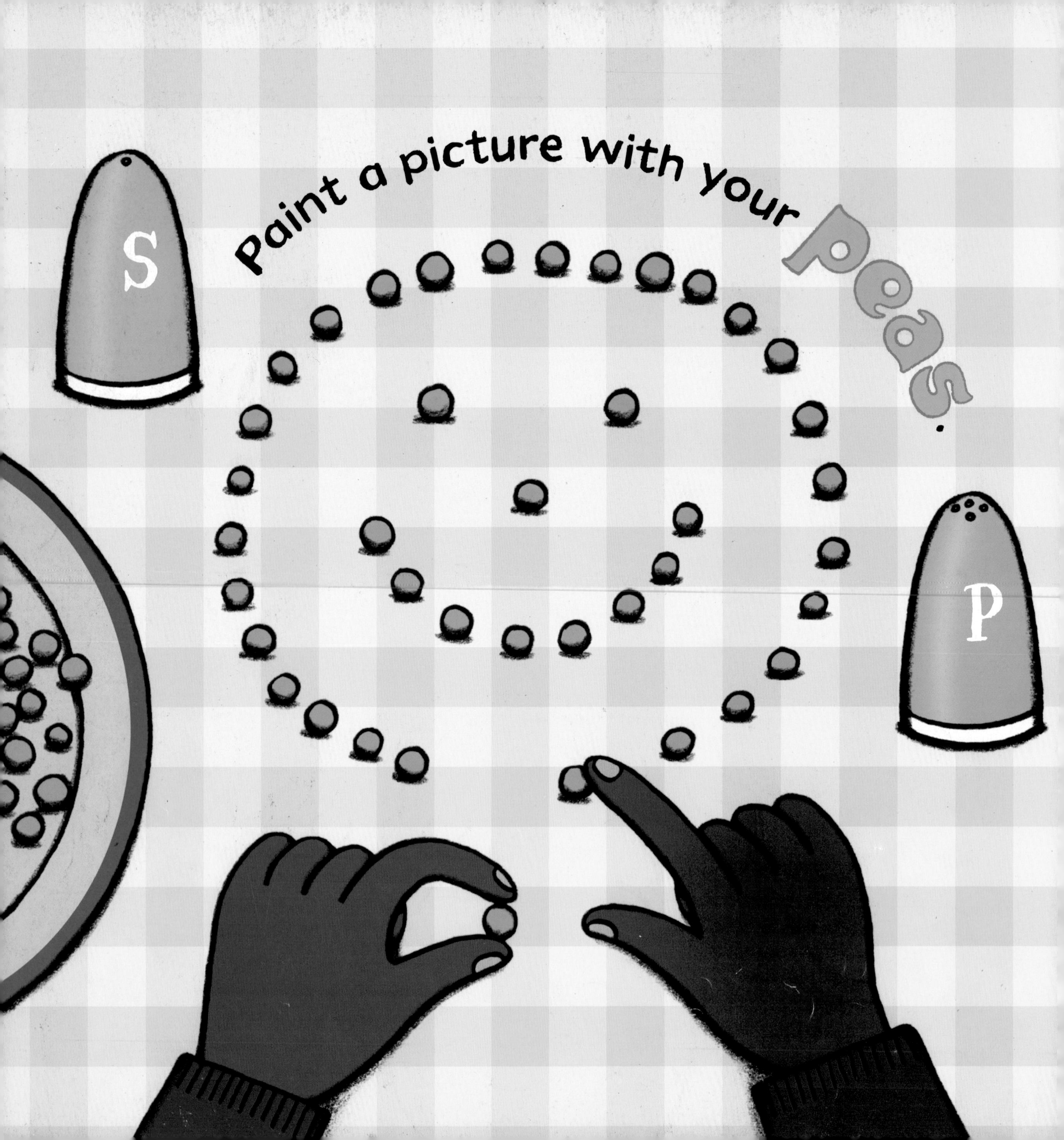

Paint a picture with your peas.

Squeeze some cheese
between your knees.

Drink your gravy through a straw.

Bounce your burgers off the door.

Bung your
thumbs in
hard-boiled
eggs.

TREACLE
Trickle treacle down your legs.

Pile up puddings on your toast.

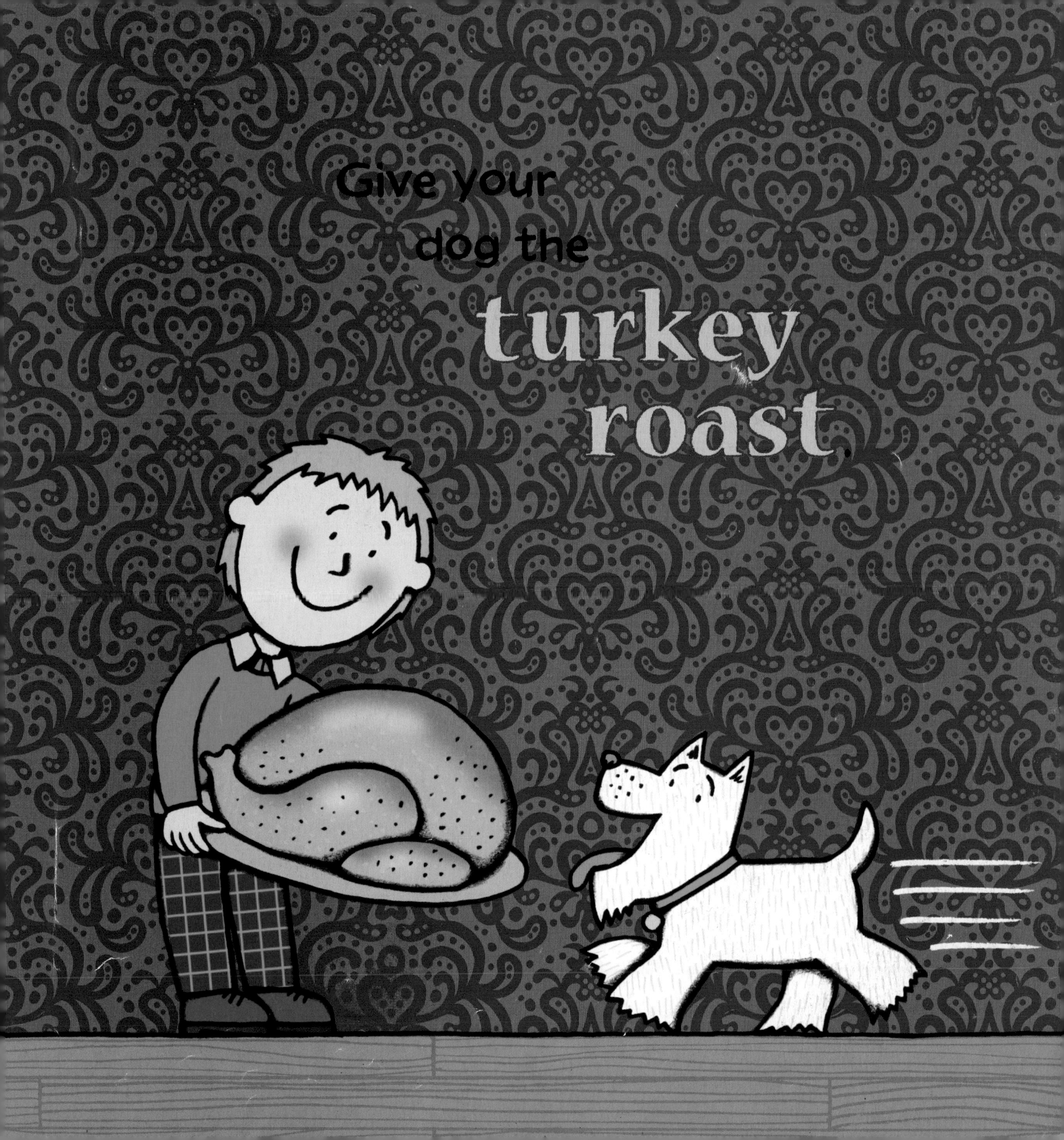
Give your
dog the
turkey
roast.

Hide spaghetti in your hair.

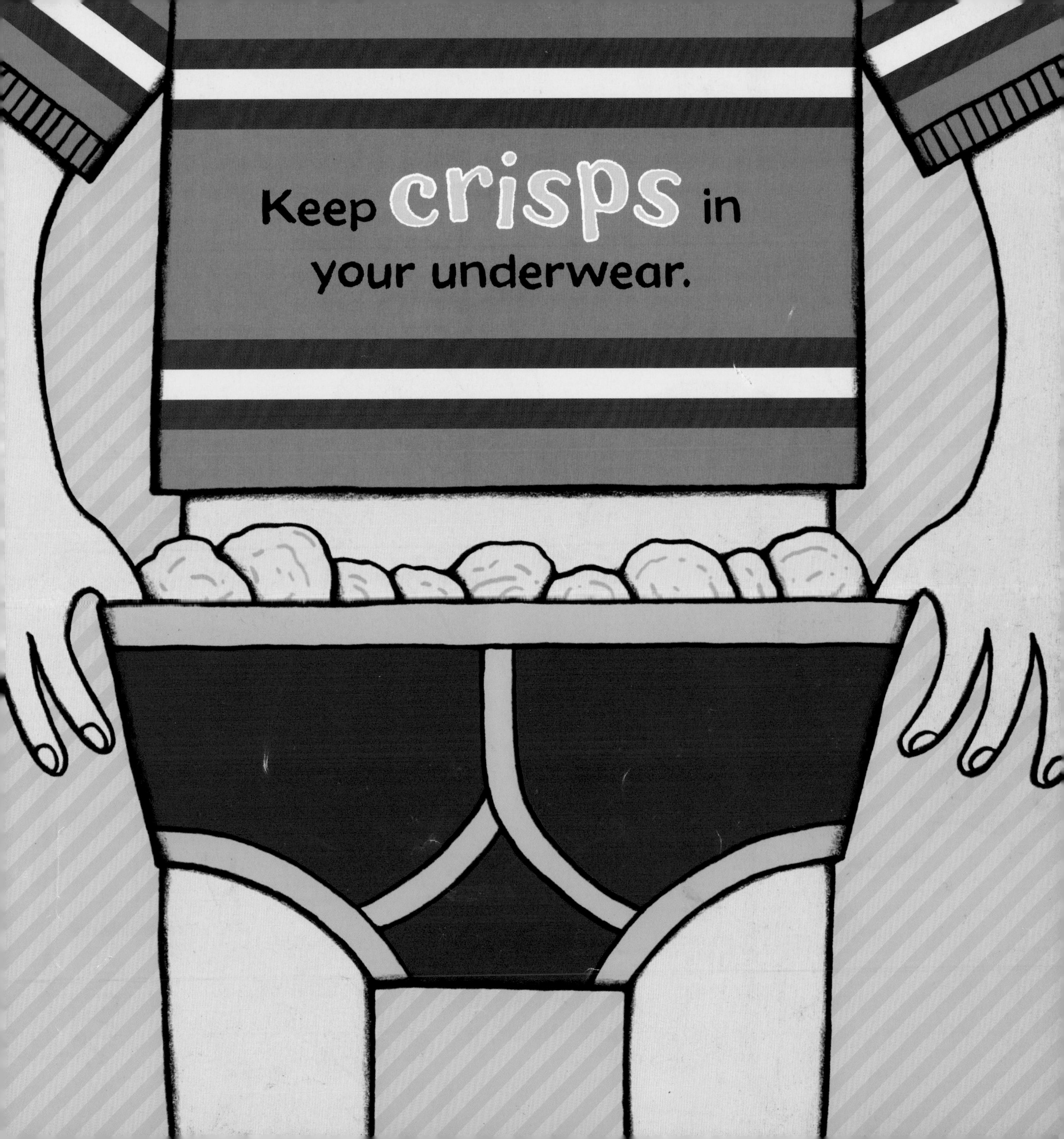
Keep crisps in
your underwear.

Juggle jelly, tread in bread.

Balance
bagels
on your head.
Wolf down waffles while you walk . . .

But never

use a knife and fork!

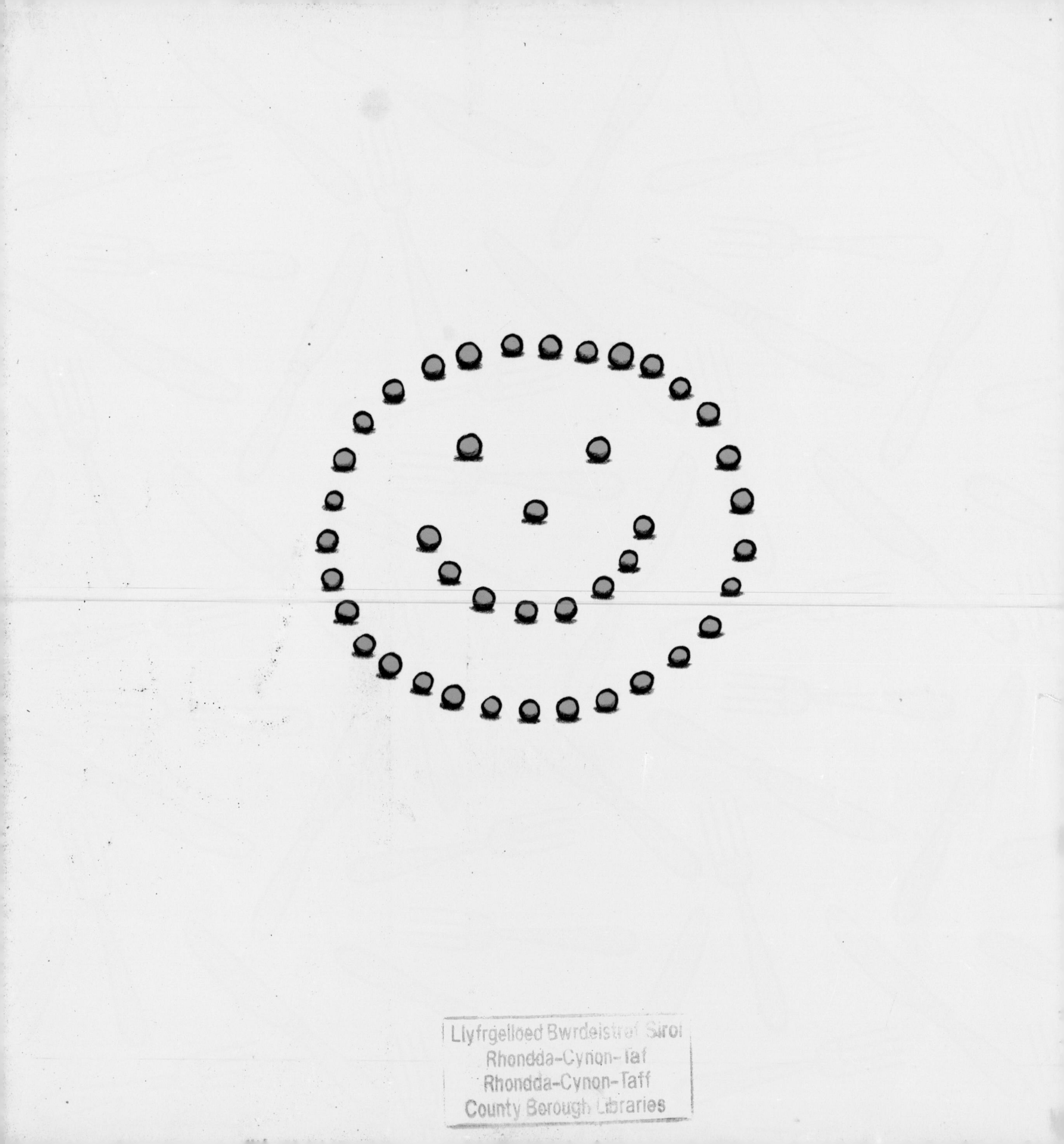